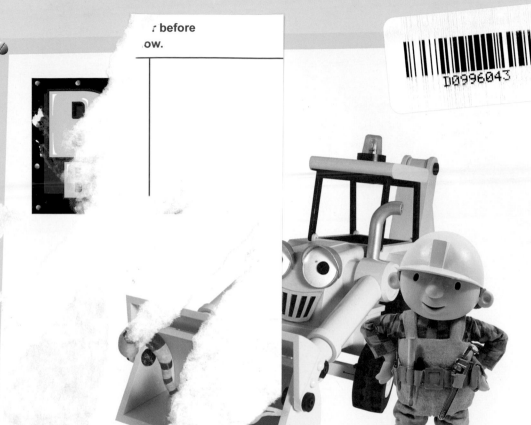

Scoop Saves the Day

It was a wild and stormy night. All across the town, thunder crashed, lightning flashed and the rain *bucketed* down.

Out in the yard, tucked snugly under Bob's lean-to, the machines snuggled together and listened to the storm.

"Ooh, Muck!" squeaked Dizzy. "This is scary."

"No, it's not," laughed Muck. "This is **fun!**"

By morning the rain had stopped and the clouds had rolled away. But a lot of damage had been done in the night – and Bob was the first person to hear about it.

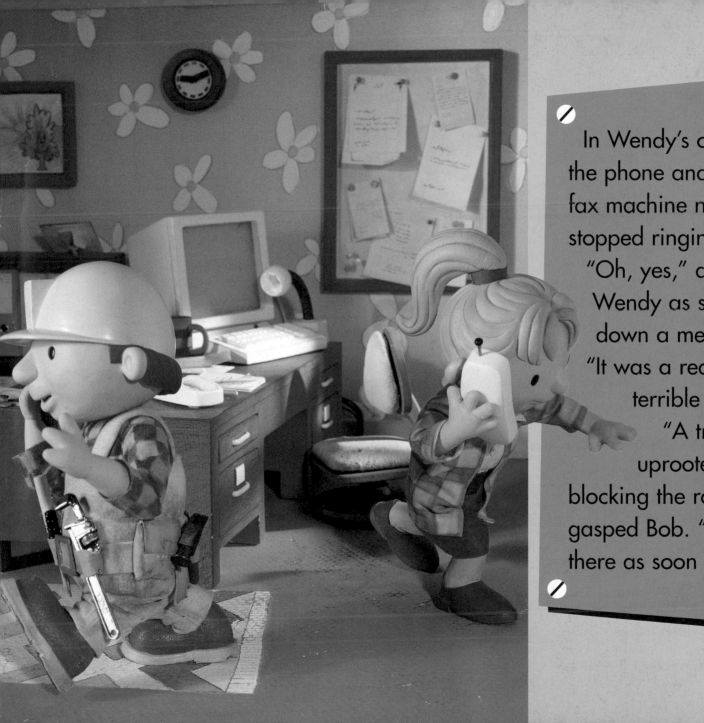

In Wendy's office, the phone and the fax machine never stopped ringing. "Oh, yes," agreed Wendy as she took down a message. "It was a really terrible storm." "A tree uprooted, blocking the road!" gasped Bob. "I'll be there as soon as I can."

Then a fax came through from the town council.

"Bob! This is urgent," said Wendy, reading the fax out loud. "Roads blocked, telegraph poles down, pipes burst and fences broken. Need immediate help!"

"OK, Wendy," said Bob, handing Wendy his mobile phone. "I'm on my way!"

He hurried out to the yard.

Wendy held a phone to each ear.

"Hello... hello! Bob will be with you just as soon as he can," she promised the worried customers.

"Hey, that was some storm last night," rumbled Roley when he saw Bob crossing the yard. "All that thunder and lightning. **Wild!**"

"It was," Bob agreed. "And it caused a lot of damage. We're needed right away!"

"I can shift it," revved Muck.

"I can mix it," squeaked Dizzy.

"I can dig it," chugged Scoop.

"I can **rollll** it!" rumbled Roley.

"And, er... I can lift it," Lofty clanked.

"What a team!" said Bob proudly. "Scoop, come with me to check out the roads. Muck and Lofty, I'd like you to pop up to the farm to make sure everything's all right there."

"Aww, what about me?" grumbled Dizzy.

"Don't worry," said Bob. "I'm sure you're all going to be needed on a day like this!"

Lofty and Muck left the yard, along with Pilchard, who went for the ride. They drove down the winding country lane that led to Farmer Pickle's farm.

When they arrived, the machines found a terrible mess. The duckpond was full of rubbish left behind by the storm.

"Quack! Quack!" squawked an unhappy mother duck and her three ducklings.

Pilchard hopped off Lofty and went to take a closer look.

"Don't scare the ducks," worried Lofty, as Pilchard crept close to the water. "They don't look very happy."

Muck chuckled. "They will be when we've cleaned up their pond! C'mon, Lofty!" he cried, as he whizzed down the hill.

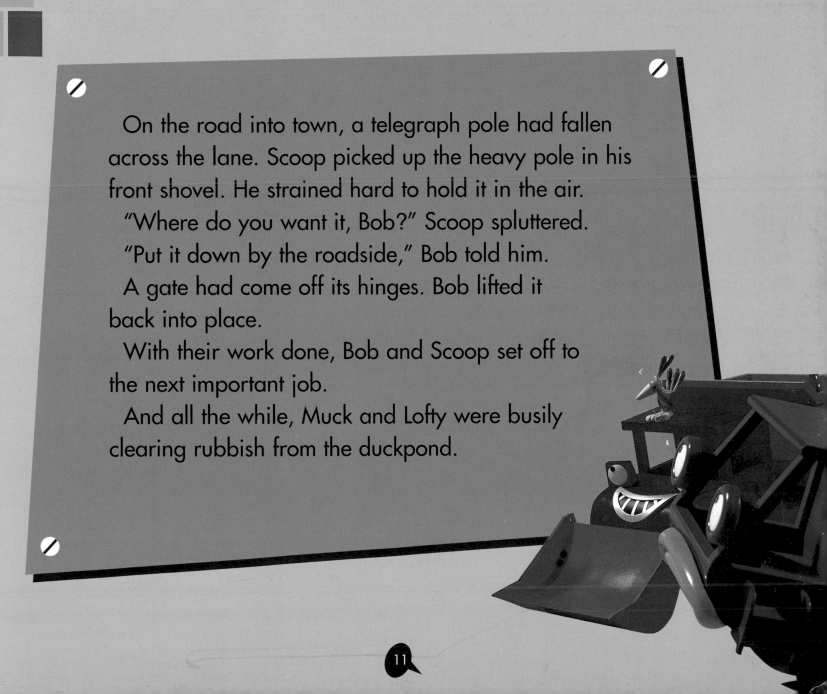

On the road into town, a telegraph pole had fallen across the lane. Scoop picked up the heavy pole in his front shovel. He strained hard to hold it in the air.

"Where do you want it, Bob?" Scoop spluttered.

"Put it down by the roadside," Bob told him.

A gate had come off its hinges. Bob lifted it back into place.

With their work done, Bob and Scoop set off to the next important job.

And all the while, Muck and Lofty were busily clearing rubbish from the duckpond.

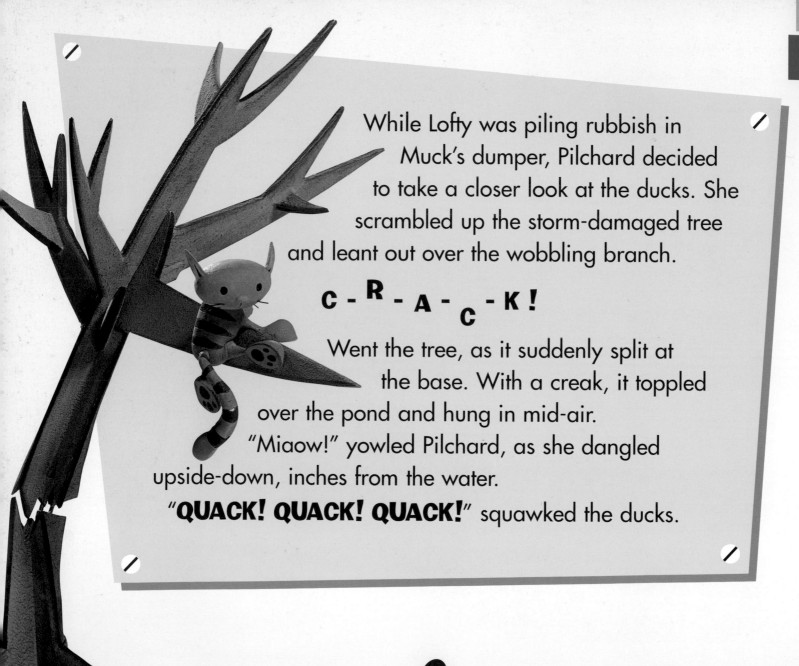

While Lofty was piling rubbish in
Muck's dumper, Pilchard decided
to take a closer look at the ducks. She
scrambled up the storm-damaged tree
and leant out over the wobbling branch.

C - R - A - C - K !

Went the tree, as it suddenly split at
the base. With a creak, it toppled
over the pond and hung in mid-air.
"Miaow!" yowled Pilchard, as she dangled
upside-down, inches from the water.
"**QUACK! QUACK! QUACK!**" squawked the ducks.

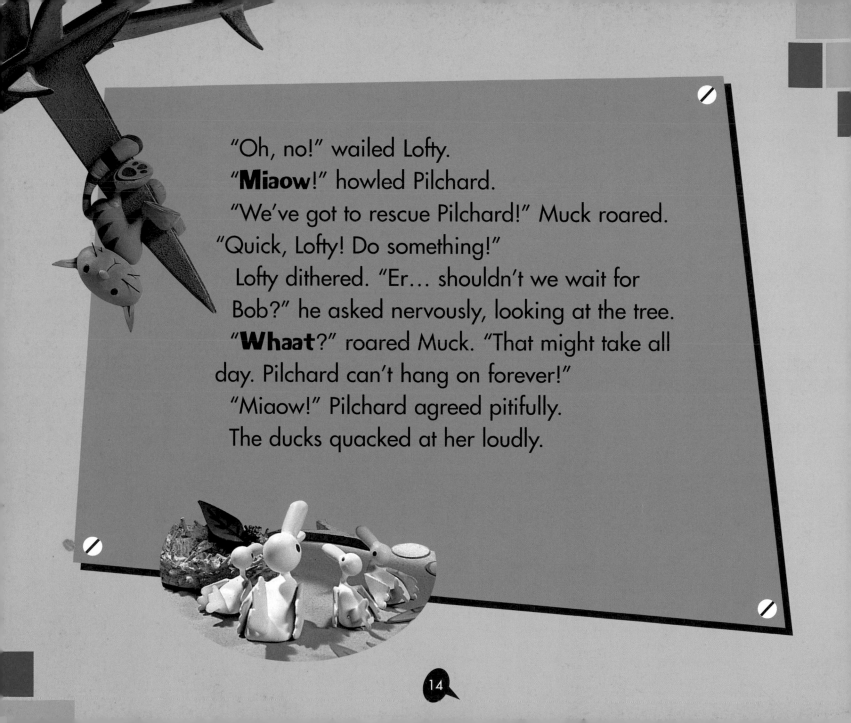

"Oh, no!" wailed Lofty.

"**Miaow**!" howled Pilchard.

"We've got to rescue Pilchard!" Muck roared. "Quick, Lofty! Do something!"

Lofty dithered. "Er… shouldn't we wait for Bob?" he asked nervously, looking at the tree.

"**Whaat**?" roared Muck. "That might take all day. Pilchard can't hang on forever!"

"Miaow!" Pilchard agreed pitifully. The ducks quacked at her loudly.

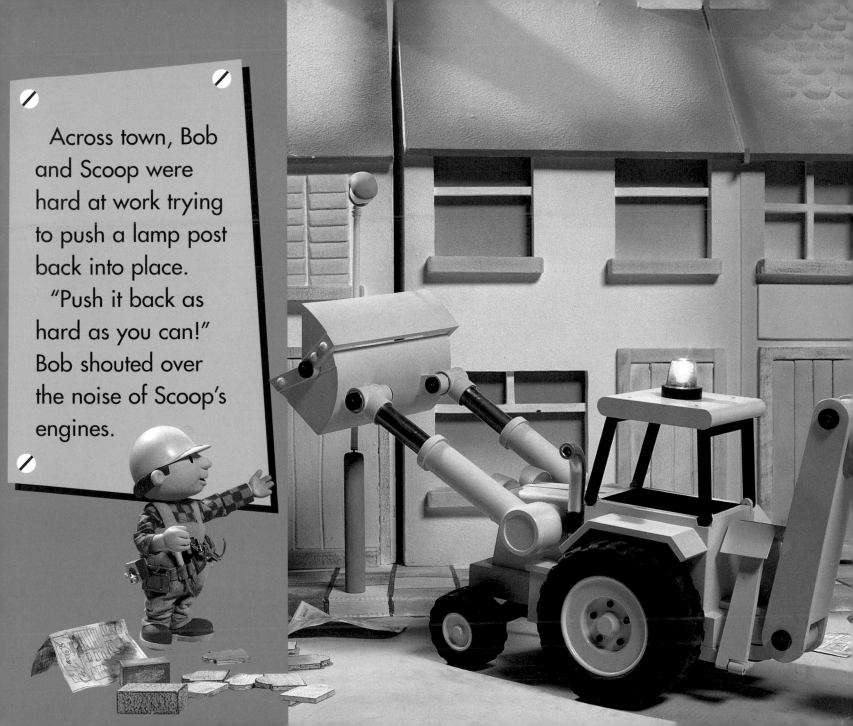

Across town, Bob and Scoop were hard at work trying to push a lamp post back into place.

"Push it back as hard as you can!" Bob shouted over the noise of Scoop's engines.

Back at the farm, Lofty was trying to hook the fallen tree. He threw his hook right across the pond, but he couldn't reach Pilchard.

"Just *grab* it, Lofty," shouted Muck.

"I would if I could!" spluttered poor Lofty.

"Cheep!" whistled Bird. He flew off.

"Bird's going back to the yard for help," said Muck.

"Should we go with him?" asked Lofty.

"I'll go back," said Muck. "You stay here and look after Pilchard."

"Help!" yelled Muck, whizzing into the yard.

"Muck!" cried Dizzy in surprise. "What's up?"

"Pilchard is stuck in a tree that's fallen over the pond. She can't swim and she hates water," Muck spluttered. "Oh, Wendy," he went on. "You've got to help her!"

"Ring Bob on his mobile, Wendy," said Muck.

"Poor Pilchard," agreed Wendy. "I'll ring Bob right away." Suddenly she stopped and stared at the phone in her hand. "Oh, no!" she cried. "Bob didn't *take* his phone!"

"One of us will have to go and get him," squeaked Dizzy.

"Wheee!" whistled Bird and zipped off. He knew *just* how to make sure Bob got back to the yard as soon as possible.

Across town, Bob and Scoop were picking up dustbins that had been scattered in the storm, when suddenly Bird flashed down from the sky.

"Wheee!" she whistled loudly.

"Bird!" cried Scoop. "What are you doing here?"

"Cheep! Cheep! Cheep!" chirped Bird, hopping up and down on the top of Scoop's roof.

Scoop listened to Bird, wide-eyed. "Bob! Quick!" he yelled, swinging into reverse. "We've got to go!"

Scoop roared back to yard. Everyone was panicking.

"Scoop! Bob!" yelled Muck.

"There's been an accident," cried Dizzy.

"A tree fell onto the pond," Muck said.

"With Pilchard in it," Wendy added. "Lofty tried to lift the tree... but it's too heavy."

"Oh, Bob," said Wendy, wringing her hands. "You've got to rescue Pilchard!"

"Don't worry, Wendy," replied Bob. "We're on our way!" He turned to the machines.

"Ready, team?" he called.

"**Can we rescue?**" shouted Scoop.

"**Yes, we can!**" chanted everyone.

With their wheels churning as fast as they could go, Muck, Bob, Scoop and Dizzy roared along the country road to the farm.

Lofty was delighted to see them power over the top of the hill. Even Pilchard perked up a little bit.

"Don't worry, Pilchard," said Bob. "We'll soon have you out of that tree."

"What about the ducks?" asked Scoop. "They'll have to move or they might get hurt."

"**Quack!**" agreed the mother duck crossly.

Putting his finger to his chin, Bob thought hard. Suddenly, he had a marvellous idea. With a big smile, he waved to Dizzy to come closer.

"See, Dizzy," he said. "I knew you'd be needed on a day like this."

Bob peeked inside Dizzy's mixer, then turned and looked back at the ducks.

Then Bob gestured to Scoop to come closer.

The digger reversed until his back bucket was above the pond.

The puzzled ducks looked at each other, as if to ask what was going on.

"I'll give you a lift up," said Scoop to the ducks, as he dipped his back bucket into the water. Very, very gently, he scooped up the mother and her ducklings.

Dizzy hurried over to meet him. Turning round, Scoop carefully dropped the ducks into her cement mixer.

"Ooh," giggled Dizzy. "You're tickling me!"

"Cheep! Cheep! Cheep!" trilled the baby ducks. They seemed quite happy in their new home.

"Now for Pilchard," said Scoop. His engines huffed and puffed as he extended his arms and held his big, metal bucket underneath the frightened cat.

"Hop in!" called Bob.

"Miaow!" mewed Pilchard, as she leapt off the branch and collapsed into Scoop's bucket.

Bob gave her a big, welcome-back cuddle. "There we are," he said, softly. "You're all right now."

Everyone was tired when they got back to the yard.

"Get a good night's sleep, you lot," Bob told his machines. "We've got a lot more repair work to do tomorrow."

"What a day it's been," yawned Wendy. "You should go and put your feet up by the fire, Bob."

"I will, Wendy. Goodnight. 'Night, all!" Bob called.

"'Night, Bob," murmured the tired machines.

When Bob walked into his front room, Pilchard was already asleep in her armchair – and snuggled up in Bob's chair was the family of ducks!

"Well, I'll be blowed!" laughed Bob.

"Purr, purr," miaowed Pilchard, sleepily.

"Quack! Quack!" said the ducks.

THE END!